SALLY NOLL

WATCH WHERE YOU GO

Greenwillow Books, New York

Gouache paints and colored pencils were used for the full-color art. The text type is Mixage Black.

Copyright © 1990 by Sally Noll. All rights reserved. No part of this book may be reproduced or utilized in any form or by any means, electronic or mechanical, including photocopying, recording or by any information storage and retrieval system, without permission in writing from the Publisher, Greenwillow Books, a division of William Morrow & Company, Inc., 105 Madison Avenue, New York, NY 10016. Printed in Singapore by Tien Wah Press   First Edition   10 9 8 7 6 5 4 3 2 1

Library of Congress Cataloging-in-Publication Data
Noll, Sally.
Watch where you go / Sally Noll.
p.   cm.
Summary: A gray mouse's journey through what appears to be the grass, rocks, and tree branches of a forest proves his mother's adage that "Things are not always what they seem."
ISBN 0-688-08498-2 (trade). ISBN 0-688-08499-0 (lib. bdg.)
[1. Mice—Fiction.   2. Animals—Fiction.   3. Visual perception.]
I. Title.   PZ7.N725Wat   1990   [E]—dc19
88-35591   CIP   AC

To my parents

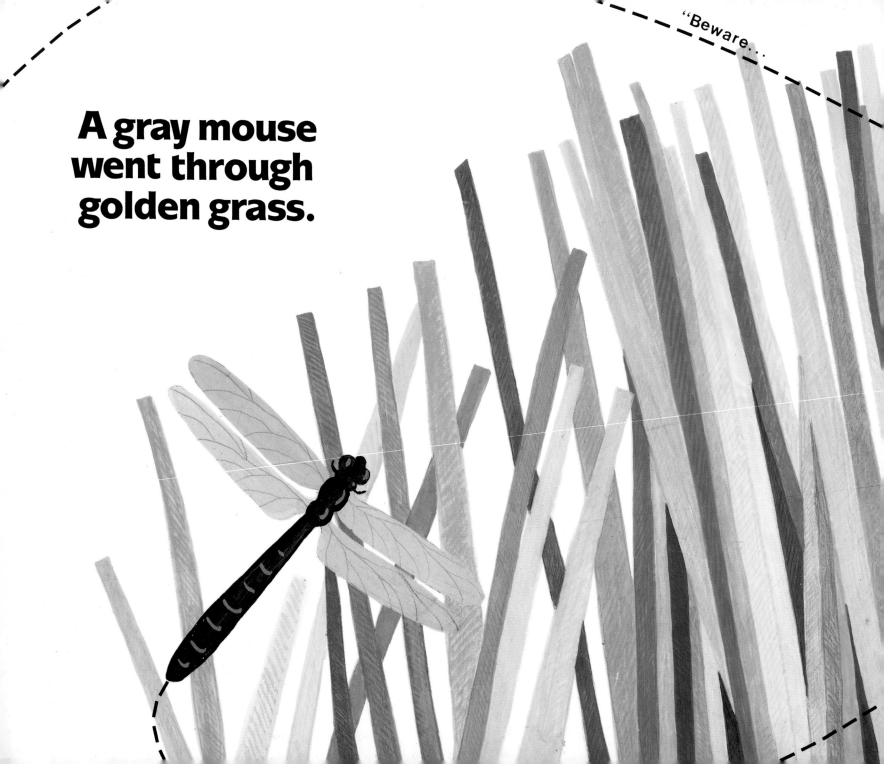

**A gray mouse
went through
golden grass.**

"Beware...

See there.....see there.....take care.....take care...

He went
up a tree,

Look out . . . . . look out . . . . . look out . . . . LOOK OUT . . . .

Too late no doubt.......too late no doubt...

along branches,

Careful....careful....scurry....SCURRY....

If I were you . . .

down vines,

Oh no......OH NO...

...watch where you go...

I told you so......I told you so...

**between rocks
and boulders,**

SHHHH.......be quiet...

Oooops...

...you must have made......a sound...

onto a bog,

Don't......OH DON'T...

...that looks like disaster...

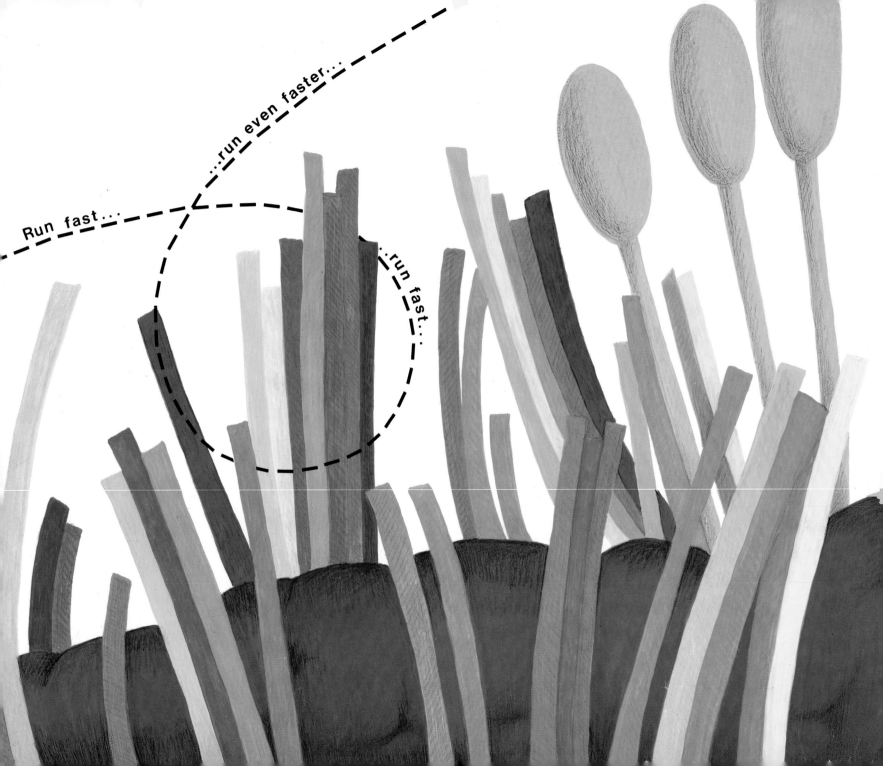

Run fast... ...run even faster... ...run fast...

into marsh grass,

Now where are you going?.....What MORE can go wrong?.

So long."

and home.